CAL AND THE AMAZING ANTI-GRAVITY MACHINE

By the same author and illustrator:
Violet and the Mean and Rotten Pirates

CAL AND THE AMAZING ANTI-GRAVITY MACHINE

BY RICHARD HAMILTON

ILLUSTRATED BY SAM HEARN

BLOOMSBURY
CHILDREN'S

Published by Bloomsbury Publishing, New York, London, and Berlin
Distributed to the trade by Holtzbrinck Publishers

Library of Congress Cataloging-in-Publication Data
Hamilton, Richard.
Cal and the amazing anti-gravity machine / Richard Hamilton ;
illustrated by Sam Hearn.—1st U.S. ed.
        p.   cm.
Summary: With his talking dog, Frankie, as a constant companion, ten-year-old
Cal Barraclough investigates his wacky neighbor's unusual experiments.
ISBN-10: 1-58234-723-9 • ISBN-13: 978-1-58234-723-3 (hardcover)
ISBN-10: 1-58234-714-X • ISBN-13: 978-1-58234-714-1 (paperback)
[1. Gravity—Experiments—Fiction. 2. Experiments—Fiction. 3. Neighbors—Fiction.
4. Dogs—Fiction. 5. Pets—Fiction.] I. Hearn, Sam, ill. II. Title.
PZ7.H182658Cal 2006   [Fic]—dc22   2005047066

First U.S. Edition 2006
Printed in the U.S.A.
1 3 5 7 9 10 8 6 4 2

Bloomsbury Publishing, Children's Books, U.S.A.
175 Fifth Avenue, New York, NY 10010

For Sara, Daphné, and James —R. H.

For Warwick, who gave me his eyes,
and Mark, who offered me his glasses, just in case.
Thank you both —S. H.

Chapter 1

Early one summer morning, as the sun slanted across the roofs of a little town, picking out steeples and chimneys and TV antennas and glinting off the blue-green wings of a flock of starlings gathered in the park, there was a sudden

CACOPHONOUS,

EARSPLITTING,

BUILDING-SHAKING,

TEETH-SHATTERING

NOISE.

CHANG-CHANG-CHANG-
EEEEEEEEEEECCCCH!

The residents of Gribbens Road groaned and pulled the covers over their heads.

"SUNDAY MORNING!" bellowed an incredulous Mr. Barraclough beneath two pillows and a comforter.

"It's six o'clock!" shrieked a tearful Mrs. Barraclough into her mattress.

This was their new house. They had been here for only two months, and they had been woken up in the middle of the night, or in the early morning, seven times.

Their son, Cal, a quiet boy of ten, was in a room at the back of the house. He got out of bed and leaned out of his window. At the back of a neighboring house, in a yard full of scrap metal, a man was operating a large piece of machinery. Smoke billowed from one end, sparks fired into the air from the other, and ribbons of shiny silver spiraled out of the side.

Cal wanted to shout at the man—but what was the point? A tidal wave of sound was filling the air.

The man looked like a giant fly. He was tall and lanky and wore oval-shaped goggles. He was feeding a long metal pole into the red mouth of the machine. His name was Frout. Mister Frout. He had long gray hair tied in a ponytail, and an oddly shaped beard that grew in a white wisp from his chin, like a dollop of Mr. Whippy ice cream. He wore blue overalls, red suspenders, and strong brown boots.

"Mr. Frout!" Cal said to himself. "Some of us are trying to sleep." His voice went up at the end as if to say, "didn't you know?"

His mother joined him. Only she took a more robust approach:

"Be quiet, you horrible, inconsiderate, thoughtless, idiotic, old CAVEMAN!" she screeched and slammed the window.

Cal looked at his mother. Mrs. Barraclough's eyes were bloodshot and blazing; her unbrushed red hair stood up on one side like a flaming bush. She closed her eyes and breathed in deeply. "I'm sorry, darling," she said loudly to Cal. "I feel better for shouting, even if the selfish old buzzard can't hear me. Why, oh why did we move here?" she groaned.

"What's he doing?" Cal asked, looking across to Mr. Frout's yard.

His mother held up her arms and shrugged. "I have no idea. The man is a menace. Just look at his yard. It's like living next to a shipyard. Mad Metal Monster Terrorizes Neat Neighborhood." Cal's mother worked as a copyeditor in a local magazine. She wrote headlines. Often she spoke in them, too.

"Why can't he wait—"

"—until a decent hour?" his mother interrupted. "It is so inconsiderate. I shall talk to the council. I will raise it with the residents' committee. I shall contact the local news. Anything to stop the torment."

"CHANG-CHANG-CHANG-CHANG-EEEEEEEEEEEEEEEECCCCH!" spluttered the machine in Frout's yard.

There was a whining noise from under Cal's bed. It was his dog, Frankie. He held his paws over his ears.

"This is driving me crazy," sang the dog. Cal understood him, but his mother didn't.

"It's driving all of us crazy, Frankie," Cal told him.

"Poor little thing," Mrs. Barraclough sympathized. "You too are suffering." She bent over and peered under the bed. "And how did you get there, you naughty boy? Haven't I told you, Cal, the dog shouldn't spend the night in your bed? It's unhealthy."

"He's not in my bed," objected Cal.

"The dog has a basket in the kitchen. The kitchen door was shut," said his mother.

"Maybe he let himself out."

"Super Pooch Opens Doors with Paws. Come *on*."

"The dog has a name," complained the dog in his gruff, growling sort of way.

"He's definitely unhappy," said Mrs. Barraclough, frowning. "Maybe I should videotape him and take it as evidence to the newsroom. Dog Nutty from Noise. Oh, boy." She held her head as if it were about to fall apart and strode out of the room.

Cal looked back at Frout.

He was feeding more metal into his machine. His features locked in a grimace of effort. The iron pole looked heavy. Suddenly, there was a change to the rhythm of the noise: a spluttering, a hiccuping of the machine. And, to the intense relief of everyone on Gribbens Road, the infernal thing chugged, swallowed—and—stopped.

Dead.

Silence.

Beautiful, blissful,

roaring, soaring

silence

returned.

The residents of Gribbens Road sank back into their comforters and pillows and breathed deeply again, groping toward lost slumber, trying to recapture escaping dreams, as birdsongs twittered again in the summer trees.

But Cal and Frankie were up. They had things to do.

Chapter 2

It had been a month since Cal met Frankie the dog for the first time. It was a meeting he would never forget. Even if he lived to be a hundred years old.

Frankie arrived in a cardboard box with holes cut roughly in the top. He had been living with a friend of Mrs. Barraclough for almost seven years, but now the friend was moving away and couldn't take an old dog with her. Cal's parents thought that having a dog would be good for a solitary boy like Cal, and there was room in their new house. The friend brought Frankie over in a box with NEW ZEALAND APPLES printed on the side and plunked it unceremoniously on the living room floor.

"Here he is," said the friend. She was a mature lady with a small hill of golden hair and a smart brown leather suit. "He's nervous and angry, so watch out."

There was a short silence, which Cal eventually filled. "Is he a Jack Russell?" he asked.

"That's right, a feisty little fella. He's a good dog—likes walking, eating, and sleeping, like all of us." The lady smiled.

Cal's mother came into the room with coffee.

"Oh, how kind—you brought apples!" she exclaimed.

"That's the dog," corrected the lady.

"Oh. Is he in there?" Cal's mother put the coffee on the floor and bent down to the box.

Her friend opened the side and a little face appeared. Frankie was white with brown eyes and a black patch across his nose. He had small, soft ears that flopped forward like little folded handkerchiefs.

"Darling dog—he's sweeeeet," Mrs. Barraclough purred. She bent over to stroke him.

"Gettorrrf," growled Frankie.

"No. He's savage," Cal's mother corrected herself, quickly withdrawing her hand.

"No, no. He just grunts," said the lady. "There never was a dog that grunts and groans like Frankie. I figure he has stomach trouble. But take no notice. The vet says he's fine—just likes to moan, that's all."

Suddenly, a loud bark erupted from inside the box:

Cal couldn't believe his ears. It was impossible. He looked at his mother, then at the lady in leather. It flashed through his mind that she might be a ventriloquist, someone who could speak without moving her lips and "throw" her voice to the other side of the room.

But both were behaving as if nothing had happened. They hadn't heard it. At least, they hadn't heard words.

"Strange noise," remarked Mrs. Barraclough, frowning.

"That's his groaning," said the lady.

With a roar, Frankie shot out of the box as if his backside were on fire. He vaulted over the sofa, crashed into the table, somersaulted in midair, and fled into the dining room.

"Whoa!" cried the lady, standing up and, by mistake, kicking the coffee over. "Whoops!" she whooped.

In the other room, Frankie tore around and around the dining room table, knocking over two chairs, then charging at the patio doors like a bull.

Unfortunately, the patio doors were shut.

He bounced back from the glass with a bone-crunching thud.

"Oh, boy!" cried the lady. "He sure is mad! I'm sorry, Linda. I've ruined your lovely carpet."

"That's fine," said Mrs. Barraclough. "Dashing Dog Causes Coffee Chaos." She smiled grimly and hurried out to get a cloth.

Cal went into the dining room. He found Frankie hiding behind the curtain. The little dog was blinking. He looked confused and angry.

Cal noticed a row of sharp little teeth.

"Ah hate boxes," snarled the dog in a voice that had an odd twang. "And windows," he added, rubbing his nose in his paw.

Cal stared incredulously. The dog was talking. In a rough, growly way, but unmistakably talking.

Frankie looked up at Cal, narrowing his eyes.

"You hearing me?" he asked gruffly, speaking out of the side of his mouth.

Cal moved slowly to the other end of the patio doors and crouched down. He nodded to the dog. All the time, he was looking into the dog's eyes. *Imagine a friend, a real dog friend.* He couldn't really believe what he had heard, but at the same time, he was willing it, wishing it to be true.

"I hear you," he said softly.

Frankie the dog looked at Cal the human carefully. His eyes took in every detail: boy, ten years old, messy, dressed in jeans and an old shirt. He had fair hair, a kind face, big teeth. No threat, Frankie decided. Maybe, even, a friend? Frankie's tail twitched a little. It almost wagged.

Cal smiled. Frankie relaxed and glanced around the room. He looked through the patio doors out into the yard. He saw the big tree at the end, the shed, and the other houses beyond. He saw a huge, bizarre metal construction, almost as high as a house, rising out of a neighbor's yard. What was that?

Then he took in the smells. The Barraclough smell (warm and a bit cheesy), the furniture polish (a sharp lemon), the dust (dry), and beyond that, burned toast from breakfast, coffee, grass, spilled ink, soap, diesel, grease and oil, and hot metal (strange) coming from that other yard . . .

At last Cal spoke.

"Hello."

Frankie seemed to think. Then he said, or rather, growled, "What's yer name?"

And from then on, Cal and Frankie were inseparable. Cal found that no one else understood Frankie. All they heard was a growly old dog with a rumbly tummy. But Cal heard about Frankie's life and his dreams and his favorite foods and his favorite walks and his favorite smells. And though he didn't really want to, he heard about all his aches and pains, and his digestion system, too. For Frankie was rather old in dog years —he was forty-nine—and his aches and pains and his digestive system were something of a concern to him.

Chapter 3

On the Sunday morning of the cacophonous, earsplitting noise, Cal got dressed while his mother went back to bed. Frankie came out from hiding under the bed and jumped up on a chair by the window.

"That man is noisy," he grunted. "That thing was so loud, it made my ears go funny. They're buzzing like bees. Your ears buzzin'?"

"No."

"Maybe I should go to the vet," Frankie mumbled. "My hearing ain't what it used to be."

"You could hear Mr. Frout though?" Cal asked.

"They could hear Frout in Fiji!" replied Frankie. "My teeth were almost shaken out of their sockets.

Maybe I should see a dentist."

"I don't think dogs go to the dentist, do they?" asked Cal.

"They can in California!" said Frankie. "Dentists, doctors, health farms, fitness centers. In California I could go shopping and have a bank account!"

"Okay. But I don't think we have doggie bank accounts here. Come on. Let's go and see what Frout is doing."

They slipped downstairs, through the stale air in the kitchen, past a table still covered in glasses and plates from the night before, and into the backyard. It was quiet there and the air was cool. They crossed the dewy grass, leaving a trail of wet footprints. Frankie led the way, scampering this way and that, his nose sniffing urgently.

He stopped by a gap in the hedge and breathed deeply. "Myrtle from Number 9," he muttered. "Out late again."

"The cat?" asked Cal.

"Yeah," said Frankie with l[...] such a tease." Frankie would h[...] chase the cat, but he wond[...] happen if the cat got away. Oh, Frankie shuddered.

At the end of the yard they ju[...] [...o the] garbage can and then up onto the wall, and from there Cal lifted Frankie onto the roof of the shed. This was where they spied on Mr. Frout. Flat on their bellies, like soldiers on a secret mission, they crawled up the roof.

"This makes my tummy tickle," whispered Frankie, his whiskers twitching.

They got to their usual spot at the top and looked out across the path to the park that divided them, over to Frout's yard.

It was a hideous mess. In fact, it wasn't much of a yard, because hardly anything grew there. Nothing *could* grow there. From end to end, Frout had laid piles of scrap metal.

There were iron girders and copper pipes, aluminum window frames, zinc taps, and brass doorknobs. There were car parts and boat parts, train parts and plane parts. There were rusting propellers and radiators and big round ...s.

...al was fascinated by this scrapyard. He longed to go over and see inside. He couldn't believe so many things were made out of metal. There was so much metal that it had grown into two towers, almost as high as the house itself. Inside these towers were passages and platforms and ladders leading from one level to another. Mr. Frout must

have spent years welding these towers together into this amazing sculpture of scrap metal. Cal often gazed at it, trying to see where things came from. Was that big chute an air vent from a factory? Or a slide from a playground? Where did that Victorian fireplace come from? And who had sat in front of it?

"Where is he?" whispered Cal, scanning the yard.

"In the tower," Frankie nodded to the tower nearest the park.

At that moment Mr. Frout came out carrying a metal pole. His goggles were pushed to the top of his head, and Cal could see his ice-blue eyes, busy calculating. He took the pole to the middle of the yard and dropped it with a clang. Then he walked around and around the pole, drumming his fingers together.

"It's another experiment," said Cal.

"Don't let him see you," whispered Frankie.

Cal nodded. You could tell Mr. Frout didn't like people. He gave the impression that he was far, far too busy to be bothered with other people. Cal's mother had waved a cheery "Hello" when they first moved in, but Mr. Frout had scowled and looked embarrassed. He might as well have stuck his tongue out.

It seemed that Mr. Frout was some sort of inventor. He spent all his time doing experiments. Crazy, weird experiments. All day long there was sawing or banging or whizzing coming from next door. Bits of metal would ping across the yard, or a machine would cough and roar. It was driving Cal's mom and dad crazy.

But Cal didn't mind. He was drawn to the yard. It was noisy, but it was fascinating. It wasn't just another yard—something was happening over there, something he wanted to investigate.

Mr. and Mrs. Barraclough closed their eyes and blocked their ears—but Cal watched and listened and learned. And what he saw was amazing.

In the first week, Frout had made a huge vacuum cleaner that could suck (with frightening force) the juice from a grapefruit or an orange. The juice shot down a glass tube into a cup on a table set for breakfast.

Then Frout invented a very noisy and complicated machine that seemed to be designed to build brick walls, but it didn't. Instead it piled bricks and spat cement at them.

Next he tried to make fireworks that exploded with fruit. The idea was beautiful, but the reality was rather messy, as bits of banana and orange and apple burst in midair and landed all over the houses of Gribbens Road.

The following week he built a "hot-water-bottle bed." It was like sleeping on a radiator (so very warm). But when Cal saw Frout in the morning, he looked pink and slightly cooked.

Every so often, Frout noticed the boy peering at him from his bedroom window or from the top of the shed. He wished he wouldn't. He didn't like children. He thought children were a nuisance.

This is what he thought: children get under your feet and trip you. They ask irritating questions. They fiddle with things. And they need looking after!

Mr. Frout's sister had children. Four whining, wheedling little brats, he thought. They had to be fed. They had to be bathed. They had to be dressed. They had to be told how to behave—not once, not twice, but hundreds of times! When Mr. Frout's sister came to visit (she came only once), she told her children not to touch anything.

"Don't touch," she said. "Don't touch." Then she said it again and again and again until she'd said it eight hundred times. Frout was cross-eyed with irritation, practically exploding with anger: the children wouldn't listen. They touched. Everything. All the time. They fiddled and poked and prodded all his things. Bah! Children!

38

And as for that boy who watched him across the path—he even had a dog! (Don't get him started on dogs . . .) And together they were watching him right now, on top of that shed.

"Don't let him see you," said Frankie again, keeping his nose below the edge of the roof.

"Hey! Look at that!" said Cal under his breath. "That is the biggest magnet I have ever seen!"

High in the air, Frout was hoisting an enormous horseshoe magnet. He secured it and then wheeled another into position below. Two more, one on each side, completed the preparations.

"That man's magnet mad," muttered Frankie.

Now Frout took the pole he had been feeding into the noisy machine earlier in the morning, climbed a stepladder, and placed it in between the magnets. It hovered in the air. It was two yards up, held by the magnetic force. Mr. Frout walked around and around, admiring it.

Then he snapped his fingers and lifted his foot, as if he were about to dance. But that wouldn't do. He didn't dance. Even when he had a great idea.

Chapter 4

"I never went to dog school, so how do I know what it is?" complained Frankie.

"I'm trying to tell you," Cal persisted. "Magnetism is a force that runs through the earth up to the north pole and down to the south pole and affects metals."

It was later in the morning, and they were once again lying on top of the shed roof. The beech tree above shaded them from the hot sun. Frankie was panting. Mr. Frout had disappeared inside the towers for several hours. Cal and Frankie had eaten breakfast, gone for a walk in the park, and returned to Frout-watch.

"Can you see magnetism?" asked Frankie between pants.

"No. But you can't see the wind either," replied Cal, not sure whether this was helpful. "It's the same force that attracts magnets to the fridge—you know the letters and things that Mom sticks there?"

"I got you," said Frankie. "So the big pole was held in the air by magnet force. What next?"

Cal didn't need to answer—for at that exact moment, there was a loud clanking sound from Frout's yard. They looked up and were confronted by a strange sight.

Out of the house strode a tall figure dressed in a shining suit of armor. It had to be Frout.

"Hey, cool. A medieval knight!"

"What's a medieval knight?" Frankie asked suspiciously.

"Hundreds of years ago, warriors would wear armor like that in battles to protect them from arrows and swords."

"Yeah?" Frankie frowned. His tongue was hanging out. He shook his head. "Must be hot in there. Good thing he's got that gap in the front to stick his tongue out!"

They watched as Frout gathered up some wires and then climbed a stepladder to where the metal pole had been. He reached the top of the stepladder and pulled the wires. There was the distinct click of a switch.

A gentle humming began.

"What's that?" demanded Frankie, as his little ears turned toward the sound.

"I don't know," said Cal, tiring of the questions. "Wait and see."

Slowly and very carefully, Mr. Frout, still holding the wires, jumped off the stepladder into thin air. The stepladder toppled over with a crash.

"Holy dog biscuits! Big bones of bison!" Frankie
stopped panting.

"Wow!" Cal breathed.

Frout was hovering in the air.

"He's going up!" Cal squeaked.

And he was. Frout was rising, very slowly, into the air. The humming was growing louder. Slowly, his arms and legs splayed out and he hovered in a star position, a full three yards above the ground. On his face there was a terrified grin.

But something surprised Frout. The suit of armor had a helmet with a visor—a metal grill on a hinge that could cover the face to protect it—and until now, the visor had been open. Only now, it snapped shut.

Everything happened at once. There was a muffled yelp as Frout's beard was caught in the helmet, like a brush trapped in a door. He jerked his arms about, trying to push the visor up again, but in doing so he let go of the wires. He immediately began to shoot up and down and then spin, as if he were stuck in a washing machine. "Uh-uh-uh-uh-uh," he grunted.

After a short cycle, he stopped spinning and was left dangling upside down. Now he looked like a medieval knight who had been thrown out of a castle window and was frozen in midair.

The visor was open, and a panting red face was visible.

"Uh," he said again.

Frankie was laughing. It was a kind of snickering—air squeaked and whistled through his nostrils, and his little paws kicked in the air. "Eeeeh. Eeeeh. Eeeeh."

"Shhh," Cal said. "I don't think that was intended. He's in trouble."

"He sure is," squeaked Frankie. "That's the dumbest thing I've seen all year."

Frout was hanging dangerously high in the air. Now that he had let go of the wires, he was stuck.

He looked at the sky, the roofs, the houses, and the trees in the summer sunshine. He looked at the wires down below that had boosted the force with an electrical current. He needed them. Now. But how?

And then, he saw the boy.

"Uh. Help. Help me, would you?" he called in a weak voice. "Now—I . . . I need the wires."

Cal and Frankie looked at each other. Should they help the Mad Metal Monster? Cal didn't hesitate. This was his chance. As he climbed down from the shed, he wondered what his mother would say. But then, she always said that he should help people who were in trouble, didn't she?

Chapter 5

Mr. Frout reviewed his situation. He was three yards above the ground, upside down, in a suit of armor on a stifling hot day. He was held there by a magnetic force, boosted by a humming core of electricity. This was exciting, uncomfortable, and now that he thought about it, dangerous, too.

Worse, he had to get a boy to help him. A boy!

Well, maybe boys were useful for some things.

"Are these the wires?" Cal asked below him, picking up two wires leading to the dangerous machine.

He would have to speak to the boy. "That's right. Pass them up."

Cal tried to reach. He moved the stepladder and climbed up, but still he couldn't reach. Frout had risen and was now too high.

"I don't think I can do it," Cal told him.

"Try pulling a wire," barked Frankie, who had decided it was wise to stay clear and sit on the wall.

Cal climbed down the stepladder. He looked up at Mr. Frout. The wires ran to a machine on the ground.

"Don't touch!" growled Mr. Frout, as if reading Cal's mind. "I know little boys—they touch. Touch everything! This experiment is delicate. Pull the wrong wire, and I'll shoot toward the ground like a ballistic missile!"

"How about you just give it a little tug?" suggested Frankie.

"A little tug?" asked Cal.

"A tug?" Frout yelped. "Eh . . ." He tried to think.

What choice did he have? It was so hot. He was steaming in this heavy armor like cauliflower in a pressure cooker. "Right. But be careful. Give the left one a tweak. Just a little tweak! This machine is quite sensitive."

Cal held his breath and tweaked. Nothing happened. He pulled a little harder. He tugged. Still nothing. So he gave the wire a big heave. Above him there was a shriek. Frout shot up.

"The other one!" he screamed as he banged his head on the magnet above him. "Orrrrrrrrr!" he groaned.

Cal pulled the other one. Hard.

Frout flew back. "Ahhhhh!"

Miraculously, he stopped only a foot above the ground.

"STOP! Don't touch," he gasped. His eyes were popping out of his red face. He held out his hands. "Give," he pleaded.

Cal carefully gave him the wires.

Mr. Frout tweaked, very gently, very precisely, on

both wires. It was as if he were flying a very sensitive kite. There was a click, and the humming stopped. The machine slowed, and Frout sank with a gentle crumple of armor to the ground.

"Back to earth," he said weakly, imagining perhaps that he was a returning astronaut. He looked up at Cal. His face twitched for a few moments, and he managed to mutter, "Thanks."

"That's okay," said Cal lightly. He looked around at the yard. He felt small among the piles of hard, strong metal. The towers cut out the sun, and the air tasted of oil.

Frout was struggling to remove his helmet. He pulled and pushed and twisted. Cal wanted to help, and felt he ought to, but wasn't sure how. Frout began to curse about rotten, useless, medieval armorers. About idiotic, stupid designs. About shoddy workmanship.

Then he stood and clasped the helmet in both hands and pulled. He let out an enormous grunt, jumped in the air, and sat down again.

"Can . . . can I help?" Cal managed to say.

Frout turned his ice-blue eyes on him: *You? Help?* they seemed to say.

"Tell him there's a buckle on the side," Frankie said from the wall.

"There's a buckle on the side," Cal told Mr. Frout.

"Ah! I might have been stuck in that for weeks," he said as the helmet came off. His hair was stuck to his forehead; his face was pink and glistening.

"You could have been stuck in the air, too," Cal told him.

"Yes," Frout nodded. "I could have." He frowned

54

EXPERIMENTATION!

and rubbed his brow and looked deep in thought. Then he brightened. His face creased, and he actually smiled. He turned to Cal and looked him up and down, as if he were seeing him for the first time. "Experimentation! You've got to experiment, and you've got to take risks. That's what I say. Now, I'd better go and change," he said abruptly, and he clanked off toward the house.

Cal looked at Frankie lying in the sun on the wall. Frankie opened an eye. "We've got a live one here," he muttered.

"He's not so bad," Cal spoke softly.

"Whaddayamean? He's a fruitcake," said Frankie.

Cal looked around the yard. He relaxed. He was struck by how many things were kept here. There was a bank of little boxes all neatly labeled. Shelves with jars of nails and screws and hooks. On the ground floor of the tower, there were tools hanging up, carefully arranged. It looked like a great big messy scrapyard from a distance—but in fact it was surprisingly organized, when you looked closely.

"Hello again," Mr. Frout reappeared at the back door in his overalls and red suspenders. Cal noticed that he waved his arms around nervously when he talked.

"As I was changing just now, I, er, had an interesting idea. I'm not used to having guests but"—and here his arms waved in a circle—"how would you like to try the world's first pneumatic milkshake?"

Cal smiled. Any milkshake was okay by him, even a—

"Pneumatic," Frout repeated. "Spelled with a silent P. It's compressed air, like the air you put in a bicycle tire. I keep it all over the place. And just now, it struck me that if I blast milk, banana, and honey with a force twelve hurricane of compressed air, it could be, well, tasty."

"Will it be full of air?" asked Cal.

"Maybe. Maybe light as a cloud."

Mr. Frout went inside and fetched an enormous glass jar as well as some milk, bananas, and honey. He poured the ingredients into the jar and fixed a sturdy rubber plug into one end. He fiddled about for a bit, clamping the glass jar into place, and fetching a wiggly pipe, which he fixed into the plug.

"Take cover," he advised. "It's possible the glass jar will explode."

Frankie scampered to the end of the wall. Cal took cover behind a car door. Frout strode up and down, checking things and rechecking them. He was absorbed in his work. At last he retreated, put on some goggles, and flicked a switch.

There was a terrific *whoosh*, and the jar turned white with milk as the contents were blasted with the compressed air. After thirty seconds, Frout turned off the air.

"Come on," he waved to Cal. "I have a good feeling about this one." He walked over, rubbing his hands.

They took the lid off the jar and peered inside. There was a glorious yellow froth, and a fine banana smell wafted up. Frout tried to tip the contents into a cup. But the froth stuck there.

"It's all froth!" Cal grinned. "Banana froth!"

"Hey! That's a first!" cried Frout delightedly. "I'll fetch some spoons."

He went off and returned with three spoons and they dug into the world's first Banana Froth. It was delicious . . . although it did have a tendency to make them burp! It struck Cal how generous it was of Frout to include Frankie. They took a spoonful over to him on the wall. Cal decided he really liked Frout. It was surprising how quickly you could make friends. How wrong you could be about somebody.

Mr. Frout was thinking something similar. How wrong he had been to think that all children were irritating brats. This one was pretty good company. Not only that—he was smart. He looked like a reliable sort of fellow. In fact, thought Frout, he would make an excellent assistant.

Chapter 6

"You *what?*" asked Mrs. Barraclough. "You did *what?*" Sometimes there seemed no halfway mark on the dial of Mrs. Barraclough's temper. She went from zero to ten in a second.

"He was stuck, and I helped him, and then we talked, and he's really very nice."

"But you don't know him!"

"Yes, I do. He's a neighbor."

"A *neighbor* doesn't mean that you know him! Haven't I taught you anything?"

Cal was silent. His mother was silent. Cal tried a different approach. He softened his voice. "I'm sorry, Mom. He needed help. And he really was nice."

"Ah." His mother was cooling down. "That's something, then. Nasty Neighbor Turns Nice." Luckily, Cal's father called at that moment and Mrs. Barraclough was distracted. Cal slipped into the yard and made himself scarce.

For the next week, Cal and Frankie watched Mr. Frout and his experiments. Cal waved to him but didn't go over. He tried to think of some of his own experiments and started a notebook with diagrams of his inventions. Drawing them was fun. Actually making them proved to be trickier.

He started with some small things:

A vacuum cleaner that sorted the things it sucked up into different sections—dust, small toys, jewelry.

Then he invented an "umbrella-walking stick-stool-sword-flashlight-ladder" all combined.

He designed a cell phone that combined a handwarmer, an electric whisk, and a secret pack of playing cards.

His favorite design was the very ambitious and complicated, "getting-dressed-and-eating-breakfast-while-watching-TV-and-finishing-homework machine." It did everything for you.

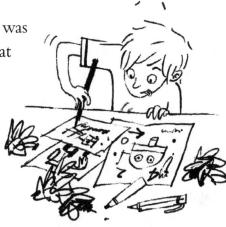

His second favorite was the "sink assistant" that would brush your teeth, wash your face and hands, and dry you, without your having to lift a finger.

And, for Frankie, there was a "doggie exerciser," complete with a cat to chase, sticks and balls to catch, and a bone to dig for—all in the comfort of your own home and taking up a minimum of space.

Cal wondered if he should show them to Mr. Frout.

Meanwhile, Mr. Frout was busy with his own designs. He was arranging magnets and mirrors and a huge rubber band that spun around and made sparks of electricity fly from a large silver sphere.

One evening, when the air was very still, Cal noticed Frout's yard covered in fog. It was extraordinary because nowhere else was foggy. There was a new chugging noise, too, interspersed by cracks.

"Mr. Frout!" called Cal from the top of the shed when he was unable to contain his curiosity any longer.

Frout's head popped out of the blanket of fog.

"What are you doing?"

"Hello. Everything's fine," he said, and he disappeared.

It was an unsatisfactory answer, but Cal let it go.

"He's what you call unsociable," Frankie jabbered, chewing on a stick. "He doesn't like society. You know—people, dogs, that sort of thing. He's a guy who likes to be on his own. The secretive type."

"I suppose hiding under a cloud is sort of secretive," Cal agreed.

"It sure is pretty, the way it just sits there." Frankie drooled, dropping the wet stick for a moment. "Maybe when the sun goes down, it'll turn pink."

"Come on," said Cal. "Let's go over. We can say we were worried about him. Mom's working upstairs. She won't know."

As they jumped down from the shed and scrambled over the wall onto the ground that separated the yards, a flash lit up the fog. It was like lightning in a cloud.

"Cal," said Frankie in a guarded tone, "I ain't so sure it's such a good idea to go in there."

Cal paused. "Okay. We'll call out."

He ran over to the wall and scrambled up until he could lean his arms on the top.

"Mr. Frout? Are you okay?" he called into the fog.

"Yes," called a breathless and excited voice. "It's pretty lively in here. I think I'm on the verge of something big. Something enormous . . . enormously big." His face rose out of the fog. He was grinning. Cal noticed his big teeth and the beard, now split into two thin ice cream squiggles. He found Frout's excitement a little alarming.

"I am finding a very strange force at work," Frout confided breathlessly. "It is as if, as if . . . as if I have gotten rid of, of, of, of gravity," he babbled. "Things are lighter, somehow. Heavy things are light and light things are . . . floating."

Cal frowned. Frankie coughed. It all seemed a little unlikely.

"If only . . . " Frout went on, jabbering, "I could . . . could . . . " His voice trailed off. He looked at Cal and then at Frankie. Suddenly his eyes grew wide as he looked at the dog.

"I wonder," he said. "Would it be a good idea, I mean, if we, he, the dog there, he . . . "

Whatever it was, Cal thought, was probably *not* a good idea.

Frout tried again. "If I have found a new force—the opposite of gravity—then I need to test it, not just on metal and wood but flesh, to see if it would work for us. And maybe if I could put your dog—"

"NO WAY!" shouted Frankie, and he sat down firmly in the path. "You cannot expect ME to be up for animal experimentation! I am against it! Obviously! If you're so interested in experimenting, YOU do it!"

Cal looked at Frout—but Frout read his expression. He held up his hands. "You're right. What am I thinking? It's a terrible idea. Poor little mutt."

"Why don't you do it?" suggested Cal.

"Well—yes, but I need help. I can't operate the machine and be the subject of the experiment at the same time."

"Can I help?" Cal asked.

Frout beamed. "Will you? Yes. Thank you. Come over." And he disappeared.

Cal dropped down to the ground. "Are you coming?" he asked Frankie.

"No," said Frankie. "I am not. I'll wait for you here." He stuck his nose in the air, independent and offended.

"Okay, that's cool." Cal climbed the wall and dropped into the fog on the other side.

The fog was thick and very cold. Cal wished he had a sweater on. He held out his hands and carefully walked forward. "Hello!" he called.

"Over here," Frout's voice came through the fog. Cal found him crouching down, fiddling with a set of levers. He looked like a wizard, ancient and mystical.

"Take hold of these levers here. They've got little lights on top, see? Green for go, red for stop. Blue controls the magnetic and static electrical mix."

"How does it work?" asked Cal.

There was a long pause.

Frout seemed to be battling with the answer.

"I . . . I don't know," he said at last. "I wish I did. It's something I can't explain, something to do with metal. It's as if there is a force here that has altered the magnetic force. Changed it into something that eliminates gravity! Wipes it out. It's just chance that I stumbled upon it—but I have, and . . . are you with me?"

"Not really," said Cal, baffled.

"Well, think of it this way: everything in the universe has an opposite—black has white, light has dark, silence has noise . . . and, somehow or other, I seem to have found the opposite of gravity—which, until now, has never had an opposite! There." He stood up. "Now, when I give the signal, pull the green up, then slowly ease up the blue. I'll be over here to see if I can feel the power."

"Okay," said Cal. He watched Frout disappear into the fog.

"Pull!" called Frout from across the yard.

Cal pulled. A hum pulsed around them and then a bolt of lightning crackled past, making Cal jump.

"The blue!" cried Frout excitedly.

Cal searched for the blue light. He was feeling a bit funny. He found the blue lever and pushed it up.

Immediately a double bolt of lightning shot past him and a vibrating hum swam dizzily around. Cal giggled. It was as if someone were tickling him. He felt light and he heard Frout laughing, too, across the garden, above him.

That was when he realized—Frout was in the air. Above him. Floating. For some reason it struck him as very funny indeed.

Then, through the laughter, he heard Frankie barking. "Turn it off, Cal. Turn it off!"

Cal pushed the red lever. The humming stopped, the chugging of the fog machine died, and the lightning fizzed weakly. The laughter in his head drained away, too.

There was silence.

"Unbelievable," squeaked Frout, to Cal's left.

Cal went toward the voice. Frout was lying on the ground, laughing.

"I was rising in the air. Astonishing!" he exclaimed. He gazed at Cal. "The possibilities for this invention are huge!" he whispered, looking suddenly serious and madder than ever. "Missiles! Missions to Mars! Giant vegetables! Oh, Cal, thank you for your help. I must go immediately. I've got work to do."

And he vanished into the fog.

Chapter 7

Frout disappeared for days. In the meantime, Cal thought about the loss of gravity. What would it mean? He looked in books and on the Internet and tried to imagine what the world would be like if everything were weightless.

He thought of floating to school, of being able to kick a football several miles, of lifting something really heavy (a car, for instance) with just one hand! Life would be totally different.

"Keep your feet on the ground," Frankie told him. "I don't want to run a mile to fetch a football. Maybe you imagined it, and Frout didn't float at all."

But Cal disagreed.

What would his schoolmates say if he and Frout had discovered a force that was the opposite of gravity? You could win the Nobel Prize for that! He imagined winning the Nobel Prize. He could float down to collect it and make a speech about the trials of experimentation, bobbing above the podium.

"I wish you were trying to invent the perfect dog basket," Frankie told him. "One with a water mattress and some bone-flavored wicker to chew. And for the older dog, something special to calm the stomach after one of those indigestible dog biscuits you owners are so fond of."

Cal laughed. "What about one with a nice scratchy blanket with stinky dog smell all over it— a basket that could take you for a walk twice a day."

"And didn't say 'heel' all the time," added Frankie.

"And would let you chase rabbits," suggested Cal.

"And would take you where there were some rabbits to chase!" Frankie muttered, tucking his head between his paws. He closed his eyes. Time to dream.

As Frankie dreamed of perfect dog baskets and rabbits, Cal dreamed of returning to the machine Frout had made. He wanted to see what it was like to float.

But Frout was nowhere to be seen. He had been gone for two days. His metal yard was silent. His house was shut up. His rusty old truck had gone. Where was he?

"Hey, nice and quiet," said Cal's father, raising his glass one evening when it was warm enough to sit outside.

"Barracloughs Bask in Balmy Bliss," cooed Mrs. Barraclough.

Cal slipped away to his room. It looked like his parents were about to get sappy. He opened the window to get rid of the stuffy air, and that's when he saw Frout.

He was wheeling a huge nest of copper wires, some more giant horseshoe-shaped magnets, and some mirrors into position. He was up to something. Cal watched as he arranged them all, and dusk slowly fell.

"First thing in the morning, Frankie, we're going to go over and see him."

"If you insist," yawned Frankie, dozing on the bed. Cal looked at Frankie. How was it that dogs could doze and talk at the same time, he wondered. Frankie sighed. "I'm not going in, though. I don't want to be part of an experiment."

But as Frankie trotted downstairs to his basket for the night, Cal thought to himself: *I do. I want to go in and be part of the experiment.* And he fell asleep thinking of that excitement and how to ask Mr. Frout if he could help.

But he woke too early, and it was still night. Watery moonlight filtered through the gap in the curtains. Cal got up to look out.

The first thing he saw was a thin layer of mist. His heart jumped. It was hanging eerily in the trees, lit by the bright moon.

Frout's yard was still. The metal towers rose out of

the mist, mirrors reflecting moonlight onto them. Frout wasn't there. Nothing was happening.

But Cal was wide awake. There was still an hour to go before dawn. He couldn't think about going back to bed now. He would go downstairs, just to look again, to get into position early, ready for when Mr. Frout came out. He wouldn't even wake Frankie.

Cal felt rather pleased with himself—he wasn't usually this adventurous.

He dressed and slipped downstairs, through the patio windows in the dining room so as not to disturb Frankie in the kitchen. He stole across the yard silently. Everything looked different in the moonlight. The world was drained of color. It felt spooky.

But when he got to the shed, he changed his mind about waiting. He wanted to take a closer look. So he climbed over the garden wall and across the path to Frout's yard. He climbed Frout's wall, too, and looked around. But he still couldn't see very well. He was so curious, he could feel his fingers tingling. He was sure that Mr. Frout wouldn't mind if he took an even closer look. So he silently jumped in.

Metal loomed around him—engine parts, wires, pipes. More wires than ever. Seeing the lights of the levers glowing like little fireflies, he went over to them and laid his hand on the green one.

This is the one Cal had pulled. His fingers closed around the lever. With his other hand, he took hold of the blue lever. In the spirit of experimentation, he could ... just ... ease ... it ... a ... little ... bit ...

The lever swung forward abruptly, and a humming began. It was a deeper, more musical hum than before. HHHUUUMMMMMMMM.

Cal panicked and pushed the blue one up. A crackle of electricity ran around the yard and, to his astonishment, his feet swung upward. He tried to hang on to the levers but couldn't, and he was swept into the air.

"Whoa!" he cried.

Frout's yard swam before his eyes. It was stomach-churning. Like a theme park ride. It felt as if it might be dangerous but, somehow, suddenly, Cal didn't care. He felt light-headed, carefree, and happy.

Up we go! he thought. *Good-bye gravity! This is what it's like to be a spaceman.*

There was his bedroom! And the roof! By the drainpipe, he saw a tennis ball he'd lost last week, when he tried to hit it over the house.

Drifting down, he passed the bathroom window. He could push off the wall—*whoooosh!*—across to the beech tree. Cal sailed through the air, tumbling gently into the twigs and leaves.

Holding a branch to steady himself, he spat out a leaf that had gotten into his mouth, and paused. He looked down at the shed and his yard, seeing it all from a new angle. He felt light and happy. This was why humans wanted to fly. It was fantastic. It was the freedom, the fantastic freedom of space that was always around us and above us, but always out of reach. Only the birds could occupy it, darting through the air. How often had he wondered what it would be like to dive and swoop like a swallow? And now, here he was. He pushed off the tree into the air with his arms out like wings. Oh! This was beautiful.

He flew gracefully down to the yard near the back door. As he approached, he brushed a lawn chair.

It tumbled over across the yard and began drifting up. Now he noticed other things drifting, too. The seat of his swing. His soccer ball. A flowerpot had fallen over, and all its contents were floating across the lawn. Without gravity, nothing was held to the ground—things were breaking free.

Then he heard a growl in the kitchen. He pushed open the back door. His mouth fell open. A wave of food was hovering in the air: pasta and cookies and cereal. The fridge door was open, and a head of lettuce flew out. Cal swam over, through the food.

It was Frankie. He was deep in the fridge, rummaging.

"Frankie!" Cal exclaimed.

"Go away!"

"Frankie!" Cal said severely. A tomato slapped into his forehead.

Frankie stopped and turned around. He had guilt all over his face—and beef stew.

"Go away! Please. I'm having the best dream of my life! I never got into the fridge before. This is heaven!"

"Frankie, it's not a dream. This is happening."

"Get outta my dream," Frankie warned. He bared his teeth at this threat to his enjoyment. "And don't be dumb. I've had food dreams thousands of times. There's a chicken in here somewhere. It always ends with a big chicken . . . "

Cal grabbed him by the back legs and pulled him out. "Look Frankie—does this happen in your dreams? Does the food float everywhere?"

Frankie looked at the food floating through the kitchen and frowned.

"Proves it's a dream, man! This ain't reality!"

"But you can feel you're floating," Cal said. To prove his point, he pushed Frankie across the room.

"Whoa!"

But he'd forgotten his own strength. Without gravity, Frankie streaked across the kitchen, his eyes wide in surprise. He swept the jugs from the shelf above the stove and bounced off the wall.

"Sorry!" cried Cal, reaching forward as Frankie came back like a pinball, nudging through assorted vegetables.

As the jugs hit the floor, they began to smash in slow motion. Shards of pottery began bouncing back into the air.

"Let's get out!" cried Cal. He took hold of Frankie by the collar and pulled him out of the back door.

Chapter 8

Clasped in Cal's arms, Frankie blinked repeatedly. He looked left and right, up and down. They were about three feet above the ground.

"Cal, is this Frout? Has he . . . ?" whimpered Frankie. "Is this the gravity thing?"

"Yes," nodded Cal. He was staring out across the yard. A cat with legs splayed out and hair on end was flying across the yard. It looked as if it had leaped from a wall and continued to travel in the biggest jump it had ever made.

And then he saw the pond. It was moving. Large bubbles of water were rising up into the air. Cal pushed his way over and stared. It was extraordinary. Phenomenal. A bubble of water!

He poked one bubble and little bubbles came off it. There were fish inside—swimming in a bubble of water.

"You gotta stop this, Cal," said Frankie sternly. "This ain't just a bit of fun. This is serious. This has upset the natural order—terrible things could happen. My stomach is doing cartwheels."

"It's amazing. And wonderful things could happen, too," said Cal, marveling at everything around them. "Think how we are squashed by gravity all the time. We could fly. We could float everywhere. There's a whole new world up here. Like Frout said, without gravity, plants would grow huge—we could have tomatoes like soccer balls. Big bushes of broccoli! Everything would be bigger. Trees, people, dogs!"

"I don't want to be bigger. I like being small!" exclaimed Frankie.

"And we could move things really easily. Without gravity, rockets could fly into space without using all that fuel. They could just push off the earth and they'd be there. We could explore the stars. You could go to the moon with a push. Just imagine."

"So what?" Frankie barked. "Imagine trying to eat your dinner with the food flying off your plate, or having a bath with the water floating around in the air, or playing cards when they won't stay on the table. Oh boy, what happens when you go to the bathroom? This is a recipe for chaos!"

But before Cal could reply, there were shouts from Frout's house.

Out of the upstairs window, Frout came tumbling, head over heels. He looked as if he were having a fight with his robe as he tried to put it on. The arms wouldn't stay still, and the top wouldn't come down. First he had it on backward, then he had it on upside down, tangled up in his nightshirt.

Floating through the air, he looked like a Victorian ghost, with staring eyes and wild gray hair.

Cal stayed still. Maybe Frout wouldn't see him. Cal knew he should never have pulled the levers, and an awful feeling of guilt washed through him. He expected Frout would be furious. But, to his surprise, Frout began to laugh instead.

He kicked his long legs out like a baby. He did a somersault, a cartwheel in the air, a dance!

"Oh, please," muttered Frankie. "I hate grown-ups dancing."

"Mr. Frout!" called Cal. Holding Frankie under his arm, he pushed off the ground and rose toward the inventor.

Frout beamed. "Cal! This is astonishing!" he squealed. "I feel like laughing, like singing, like jumping for joy. I'm flying! Come with me, Cal."

Frout grasped Cal's free hand and pushed off from the metal tower, pulling them gently down toward the ground.

"We are in a bubble of zero gravity. Look at the way the trees and bushes are moving. It's as if they're underwater. I feel light and free and strong. I could run a thousand miles! I could spit a thousand miles!" He picked up a heavy anchor with two fingers. "Look: it's as light as a feather." He grinned and blinked. "Beautiful." He sniffed.

Cal wondered for a moment if Frout were going to weep.

"Hello, dog," he said to Frankie. "You are the first dog to be in zero gravity on earth," he told him. "How do you like it?"

"The dog has a name," growled Frankie.

"He's not sure," said Cal.

"Oh. Well, it will take some getting used to, I suppose. Now, let's check out this machine." Frout began examining wires and dials and mirrors and magnets. He was so excited, he could barely concentrate. He kept throwing his arms in the air and sighing and shaking his head and laughing.

"Inside this bubble of zero gravity," he explained to Cal, "there is this house and your house and the gardens and a slice of the park. Beyond that, everything's normal. But," his eyes glinted, "imagine: what if the whole world were in zero gravity? Eh?"

"I don't know," Cal replied. "I think maybe, you know, that might be a little much."

"Oh?" Frout twisted his beard around his forefinger. Cal saw how it got its distinctive wavy pattern.

"Look, Mr. Frout, the sun's coming up."

Frankie barked. "Hey. Look out, guys!" he warned. "Everyone's waking up."

"Ouch!" Frout looked down. Something stung him.

At the same moment, Cal felt it, too. "Ow!" he rubbed his leg.

Suddenly, the air began to fill with insects. Flies, bees, beetles, earwigs, greenfly, blackfly, moths, and butterflies began to rise into the air in a crazy cloud. Everything that flew seemed to be changed and confused by the loss of gravity. They couldn't fly properly anymore. Insects buzzed and fizzed and whined around and around.

"Ahhh. Yuck!" cried Frout, waving his arms.

"Ugh!" Cal spat out a moth. Frout scratched his hair then grabbed his nightshirt at the bottom. "Orrrr! They're swarming. Right up my shirt!" he cried.

"Gettorf!" yapped Frankie, kicking out and twitching his tail.

The insects flew in strange patterns, looping and zigzagging unnaturally.

"Look out!" cried Frankie. "Snails!"

On the ground a carpet of slugs and snails were rising slowly. There were worms and beetles, too.

"Everything's waking up, Mr. Frout!" said Cal.

"Extraordinary! Remarkable! Disgusting!" cried Frout, fascination and horror written all over his face. He had flies in his hair and a butterfly buzzing in his nightshirt.

"Horrible. Vile. Infestation!" he screamed, kicking out frantically.

A moment later some birds shot past them at high speed and slammed into the metal towers. More followed. They were flying like bullets, only twisting and weaving out of control.

"Look out!" cried Cal. A duck shot past with a loud "QUACK!" Feathers flew. A second later, a pigeon hit Frout in the leg.

There was a shout from Cal's house.

"IMPOSSIBLE!"

It was Mr. Barraclough. He opened the window in Cal's room and stared out. Behind him, Mrs. Barraclough floated, screaming hysterically.

"IMPOSSIBLE!"

"Quick!" shouted Cal. "Turn it off!"

"CAL!" cried his parents.

"I'm fine!" he called back with a smile. He waved to his parents, hoping that if he pretended everything was quite normal, then they might think it was. Just then a fox

spun past. Cal shrugged in a "Well what d'ya know?" kind of way.

But it was pointless. He couldn't ignore the horrified look on his parents' faces. There was no point in pretending. Everything they could see was distinctly abnormal.

He let go of Frankie near the ground and struggled over the wall to reach the machine. Small animals and insects wriggled around him. They were so itchy! Frout was squirming about, swatting insects and fending off floating debris like a madman.

"Turn it off!" Frout cried.

Cal found the levers and pulled. The humming changed. There was a high-pitched screech and a hideous sucking sound. Suddenly, Cal felt himself thrown away from the machine by a terrific force. He flew across the path between the yards, into the branches of the beech tree.

The air cleared. *Zing!* Gone. Everything floating in the air had gone. Where?

It took several moments for him to realize what had happened. Cal looked up. The insects were above them in the sky. He hung on tightly to a branch.

I'm hanging on, he thought. *I am looking up at the ground, but I feel like I am going to fall into the sky.* He looked down to his feet. Past his feet lay the sky. He felt he was being sucked into the sky.

"Are we back to normal?" he heard Frankie ask from his position under a bush on the ground.

"Not exactly," Cal whispered. "In fact, not at all."

Chapter 9

They were upside down. Instead of everything falling back to the ground, it had all fallen into the sky.

Frout was hanging on to a small tree by the wall.

"Disaster. Total disaster," he panted. "The force field has changed. We have moved from zero gravity to *anti*-gravity. This is big trouble!"

"Turn it off," growled Frankie. He seemed to be hanging on to something by his teeth.

"Can't you turn it off?" echoed Cal to Frout.

"I'm . . . ," Frout began. He looked suddenly lost, unsure. "I can't. I'm stuck," he said lamely. Cal looked from the beech tree to the ground. He saw Frout's sagging shoulders, his long wild gray hair, how he was hanging on in that ridiculous robe. And something else. Fear? "What have I done?" Frout moaned pathetically.

"Oh, boy!" Frankie sighed. "You humans!"

"Can you make it over to the machine?" Cal asked.

"I can't move," sobbed Frout. "I'm terrified."

Great, thought Cal. He looked over to the machine in Frout's yard. It was making a high-pitched humming noise. Someone, somehow, had to turn it off. If he could get to it, then he could try again.

In his mind, he worked out a route along the wall, across the gateway to the park, then along Frout's wall. Hanging on to bushes, gaps in the bricks, anything. He would have to be agile. *How I wish I were a monkey*, he thought.

Then he set out. Bit by bit, he edged his way over. He tried not to think about the gaping sky beneath him. Like a rock climber, he concentrated on each foothold and each handhold that presented itself. One step at a time. Then the next. Only when he had made it across did he look back and breathe a sigh of relief. And dare to look at the machine.

Immediately, he saw what he had to do. The main part was held by a cable to a hook in the wall. If he could unhook that, then something—he wasn't sure what—would happen. Maybe it would fall and then . . .

He reached down and twisted the cable free. With a sharp snap, the machine lurched around, swinging on one end. At the same time the towers wavered.

Cal hung on. His foot found a place by a missing brick, and his hand found a thick nail to grasp hold of. He closed his eyes and waited. He could feel something happening.

A moment later there was an earsplitting noise, a noise that drilled through his bones and shook his teeth and made his eyeballs quiver. The whole of Frout's yard—the machine, the metal towers, the sheds—all began to break free and fall into the sky. They gathered momentum, rising above the houses—shrieking metal scraping and grating and clashing together.

And then, growing smaller and smaller and fainter and fainter, they traveled farther from the earth into the sky.

The anti-gravity force had gone, pulling all the metal from Frout's yard with it. Without the force, Cal felt a familiar push toward the ground. Gravity was back. He managed to smile. *This feels better. This is as it should be*, he thought. "Gravity, keep pushing," he said aloud. He felt the warm sun on his back and the brick against his cheek. He tried loosening his grip, then he relaxed and opened his eyes. Gravity held him again to the wall.

"Look out!" cried Frankie nearby.

Cal looked over. Frankie was staring into the sky. The bugs and birds were returning!

Leaping from the wall, Cal snatched Frankie up, prying his jaws from the trunk of the bush he was under. Together, they scrambled over the wall into Cal's yard, to the safety of the shed. They hid inside and listened to the *pitter-patter thump bing bang bong buzz* of things returning to earth.

After a minute or two, when it was quiet again, they peeped out and looked up, half expecting to see the towers falling back to earth. But they were far away, sucked out to space by the force field of the machine, and the sky was a beautiful, empty blue.

They stumbled into the garden, sank onto the warm grass, and felt the earth pressing against their bodies.

"I am never going to move from here," said Frankie with feeling.

Cal looked at him and smiled with relief. Farther off, Frout was wandering unsteadily around their yard. He was following a bee, buzzing from flower to flower.

It felt dreamlike, this return to reality. It was a beautiful summer's morning again; the air was cool and scented, the birds twittered, the grass was fresh. Their world was heaven again.

Suddenly Mr. and Mrs. Barraclough erupted out of the patio doors into the yard. They were still in their pajamas and nightshirts, their hair on end.

"A Scene of Indescribable Devastation," Mrs. Barraclough said, as if she were a reporter.

"A nightmare. A nightmare," Mr. Barraclough repeated. "Have you seen our house? Destroyed! Devastated! Shaken to smithereens. Blasted to bits."

They picked up Cal and hugged him until he could hardly breathe. "I'm okay," he kept saying. "I'm okay. I just can't breathe!" Mrs. Barraclough kissed Frankie's wet nose. Then they turned to their neighbor.

"Mr. Frout!" hissed Mrs. Barraclough, pulling herself up to her full height and snorting like a horse.

Frout turned, blinking. He seemed transfixed by a rose.

"Well?" demanded Mr. Barraclough, puffing himself up like a turkey.

Frout looked at them all. They seemed to expect something of him.

"What a beautiful yard," he said softly.

"What?" Mr. Barraclough shook with silent rage. "Have you seen my house?" he demanded. He was practically clucking.

"Ah. Sorry," said Frout.

"Sssssorry?" squealed Mr. Barraclough, his eyes popping out of his head.

"Dad," said Cal quickly. "I turned it on. It was my fault."

His father turned to him. "You?"

Cal nodded.

"Made that . . . CHAOS?" he boomed.

Cal nodded again. He decided to tell his dad the extraordinary truth. "We've discovered the opposite of gravity. Well, *he* has." He pointed to Mr. Frout.

His father ran a hand across his stubble. He was a man of vision. "There's no telling where this could end," he said darkly. "Without gravity, the earth would wheel away from the sun. Life itself would be extinguished!" He narrowed his eyes. "Tell me, Mr. Frout, once science has discovered something, can you ever . . . *un*discover it?" He stared at Frout with a threatening glint in his eyes.

Frout nodded slowly. "Yes, I . . . I . . . believe you could."

"Good," said Mr. Barraclough. He had the air of a man who had struck a deal. "Good."

"Mind you," said Frout dreamily, "I was never quite sure how it worked in the first place."

Frout gazed around at the garden. "This is very nice," he said approvingly. "Peaceful."

He looked over at his own garden, at the space where the two towers had stood. Suddenly, he knew what he was going to do.

Chapter 10

In the next six weeks, Mr. Frout worked on his garden. He had trucks bring in fresh soil. He ordered mature trees and a ready-made lawn. He invented an elaborate water feature—part mountain stream, part pond, where fish lurked under lily pads and dragonflies skimmed the water.

He made a lawn with stepping stones and little pathways, with benches dotted here and there. He built a beautiful garden, and he took great delight in it.

In time, he waved to Mr. and Mrs. Barraclough, and they waved back. It helped that he had organized extensive repairs to their house and belongings.

One day after school, Cal and Frankie went to Mr. Frout's. Frankie sat by the pond admiring the new garden.

"Beautiful," he drawled.

They heard the gentle *snip-snip* of hedge clippers.

"Hello there," said Mr. Frout, appearing with a smile from behind the fountain at the head of the mountain stream.

"Hi," said Cal.

Frout sat on a nearby bench. He wore a wide-brimmed hat, a vest, a pair of old trousers, and boots. He looked different—like a gardener—relaxed.

"I never knew," he confided, "that I would get so much pleasure from gardening. You know, working *with* nature, rather than taking it apart. I've seen some gorgeous butterflies today. And, I'm thinking I might have a wild garden for the birds over there, so they have somewhere to build nests."

"Oh," Cal was quiet. "So you're not doing any more experiments?"

"Well, this is a kind of experiment. I'm experimenting with different plants, seeing how I can tame them to make a beautiful garden."

"But you're not doing any more experiments with gravity? Or with metals? Or compressed air?"

"No. I'm all done with that. Let's just say it was too exciting."

There was a silence.

"And anyway, I'm not sure that humans are ready for life without gravity. Birds and insects and animals certainly aren't."

There was another silence.

"Is anything wrong?" Frout asked.

Cal gathered up his courage.

"I was wondering, do you know where I could get one of those big magnets?"

Richard Hamilton is the author of many children's books, including *Polly's Picnic* and *Violet and the Mean and Rotten Pirates*. He lives in England.

Sam Hearn graduated from art school in London and works as an illustrator with a part-time job in a children's bookstore. He also illustrated *Violet and the Mean and Rotten Pirates*.